Samuel Greene Wheeler Benjamin

Constantinople

The Isle of Pearls and Other Poems

Samuel Greene Wheeler Benjamin

Constantinople
The Isle of Pearls and Other Poems

ISBN/EAN: 9783337409050

Printed in Europe, USA, Canada, Australia, Japan

Cover: Foto ©Andreas Hilbeck / pixelio.de

More available books at **www.hansebooks.com**

CONSTANTINOPLE,

THE ISLE OF PEARLS,

AND

OTHER POEMS.

BY

S. G. W. BENJAMIN.

CONSTANTINOPLE.

CONSTANTINOPLE.

I.

BYZANTIUM ! proud city of the sea !
Thou fairest of the fair, whose fading pride
Bedecks the Osmanlee's rich diadem !
Is there no harp to swell thy funeral strains,
To celebrate Time's gradual march along
Thy moss-grown battlements and silent halls ?
Is there no bard to lift his voice on high,
And to lament thy pristine greatness, O

1

Thou vast necropolis of darkened fame,
Of dead magnificence ? — Thou mistress old
Of tottering ruins, whose worn features still
Bear witness sad to thy primeval glory !

II.

The zephyr off the land sighs mournfully
Over the aged city's grassy roofs ;
The silver wave glides rippling up the beach ;
The high-prowed checkdemé [1] floats motionless,
Its shadow twinkling o'er the glassy swell,
Where the lone fisher-duck dives silently ;
From time to time some dweller of the deep
Leaps curving through the air, and darts again,
With heavy plunge, beneath the tranquil flood.
No voice disturbs the solitude of walls
Doomed to the earthquake and the battering surge.

Comes there no sound adown the waste of years
To strike the dreamer's ear ? — no muffled wail,
The dying notes of ages long expired ?
What mean the marble fragments strewed around,
Like whitening sculls upon a battle-plain ?
What means the dreary desolation which
Broods o'er these towers, that have no sentinel
Except the hermit stork in summer time ?

---

[1] Small coasting craft.

III.

Rise, Spirit of these Ruins, sorrowing
With moaning hollow as the voice of one
Who mutters in a mountain's riftless cave !
Awake from out thy trance of grief ! awake !
Withdraw the veil of nightshade from thy brow ;
Remove the covering off the silent Past,
As a fond mourner lifts the rustling shroud
From the fixed features of the one she loved,
And let us view the mysteries of Time.

The nations sepulchred below appear ;
Innumerably the generations pass,
With fabulous pageantry, — rich kings and queens,
Scholastic monks, and mighty men of war :
But every visage bears the ghastly hue
That speaketh of Oblivion's dolorous land.
How solemnly the shadowy train moves by,
Obedient to the roll of requiem strains !

Renowned in arms, lo ! Constantine the Great,
He of the cross-emblazoned standard, comes ;
Exulting pæans bid the victor hail
To proud Byzantium, his imperial seat.

Who passeth there, with siren glance, and locks
Tossed back disdainfully from shameless brow ?
The imperial wanton Theodora, — she
Whose charms appeased a factious populace.

The laurel withering on his temples sere,
The hero of a hundred fights draws nigh,
Who learned th' ingratitude of princes' hearts.
O Belisarius ! in an age of vice
Unsullied, to thy jealous sovereign true,
Nor daunted by thy country's threatening ills,
Thou wert a pharos firm upon the rock
When lashed by storms. Surpassing rich the race
That in its records shows a man like thee !

The champions of the Cross, marshalled in haste
From Albion's shores and Caledonia's wilds,
From gay, chivalric France, from Rhineland's towers.
And from Hesperia's citron groves, approach —
A phantom host defiling from the tomb.
Triumphant breathes their clarion symphony,
Down the past ages fainter, fainter growing,
Until the vast array is lost in gloom ;
Their waving plumes and spectral steeds are gone.

IV.

And now the wailing of a falling empire
Breaks on the ear. The noble-hearted king,
Son of degenerate Cæsars, but in soul
Last of the Romans, dies ; and, conquerors,
Fierce Islam's squadrons, like a torrent's flood,
Pour irresistible into the town.
Resounds, in yells victorious, " Allah hu ! "

Again! again! the war-cry rings to heaven,
With tambour's beat and chargers' stirring neigh!
The fair Greek maiden. nursed in luxury,
Flies, with her glossy tresses streaming wild,
Her black eyes melting with her frantic woe,
To St. Sophia's shrine; and innocent child,
And matron gray, if they may haply find
A refuge from the scimetar that gleams
Through all the streets. Ah me! how vain, how vain!
The sanctuary's spell is powerless!
The brazen portal yields unto the hordes,
Who bind their captives round the crucifix
Whose silver arms so oft before had blessed
Those victims as they worshipped there in peace.

The legend[1] goes, that when the Janizary,
With sacrilegious weapon, would have slain
The servant of the Lord, who, like the star
That brightest shines in a tempestuous sky,
Sung out the holy mass with heart and voice
Unshaken by the tumult that raged round,
A heavenly messenger snatched him unseen,
And, with the sacred Host, concealed him there
Within a secret nook. And oft since then
Strange sounds are heard in the chill masonry,
Filling the passer-by with silent awe.
'T is said, that when the Christian warrior's shout

---

[1] A tradition current among the Byzantine Greeks.

Goes up again in victory through this land,
And makes the dead man quake in his last sleep;
When the fear-stricken Turk feels suddenly
Great horror and the blackness of despair
Shadow his reeling brain, — then shall appear,
From out his long asylum, this old priest,
And. bearing yet the same unmouldered Host,
Shall consecrate again the chancel's pale,
By Infidels so long profaned : and then
The joyful anthem through these cloistered aisles
Shall peal in echo upon echo vast
Of loud thanksgiving, as it was erewhile
When King Justinian in Byzantium ruled.

V.

Now music sweeter far than combat's rude
And dissonant clangor, soothes the holy calm
Of twilight, floating starwards murmurously
As dash of waterfalls in summer woods,
Or pastoral hum of bees, — bright fountains. carved
Grotesque, spout ceaselessly their beaded spray
Into cool basins hewn of lustrous marble,
Round which the rose in clusters flings her buds,
To catch the purest drops that flashing fall.
The ghostly moonlight lingers silently
O'er the Seraglio gardens' velvet sward.
And hearse-like cypresses across the light
Throw solemn shadows.   Wreathed with lilies pale,

Fantastic forms are flitting joyously
Around the magic founts, who seem more like
Ethereal sprites that haunt this Paradise,
Than mortal creatures of terrestrial mould.
See how their silk cymars wave tremulous
Among the lilacs, as they skip the dance,
And blithely carol their melodious strains!

SONG.

With fairy-like graces,
And leaving no traces,
We hover from flower to flower,
The nymphs of this moon-lighted bower.

We toss our black tresses
To the low-sighing breezes,
And, soft as a dreamer's light fancies,
Illume the dark trees with our glances.

To the notes of our singing
The moments are winging—
Returning thence never, ah, never—
To the land of the silent Forever.

But why do we borrow
Regret from the morrow?
Since all but the present is hollow,
May love be the star that we follow.

The fragrant jasmines wave like shooting stars
In gentle cadence to the harmonies
So gayly trilled by these wild-warbling sylphs ;
And in yon neighboring halls illuminate
Festivity's perpetual revelry
Lulls to forgetfulness of his domains
The haughty monarch of these lovely realms.

VI.

Another scene appears.   The howling blast
Sweeps fiercely round the watchtower's dismal walls ;
The muffled sentinel's lone midnight cry
Along the battlements is lost amid
The deep, hoarse thunder of the rolling surf,
Whose foaming crests flash dimly through the gloom.
A noiseless group approaches, half obscured
By the storm's blackness, and their arms support
A sackcloth-shrouded corse.   Anon they reach
A gateway in the wall, from whence leads down
A creaking stairway to the angry surge.
Hist ! hark ! a heavy plunge ! — the deed of death,
The crime that no remission finds, is o'er !
Zoraya ! sweet Zoraya ! star of morn !
Pearl of the gay Harém ! — one short hour since
Thy playful accents musically rang
By fretted ceilings in the festal hall.
Thy lord, he frowned on thee, O gentle heart,
And hushed thy voice forever in the sea !

Save the shrill storm-blast's melancholy wail,
No dirge is sung for thee ; the clouded moon
Looks sadly on the cormorant wheeling round
Thy deep sea grave, and through their veil of mist
The stars shine like a maiden's drooping eyes
Suffused with tears ; for, certes, ne'er was fate,
And ne'er was burial, known so sad as thine,
Zoraya, O Zoraya ! star of morn !

VII.

Go to, thou visionary ! — thou that dream'st
These unsubstantial fancies of the brain ! —
Seek not to weave the Present with the Past, —
A union that can find no favor in
These busy, hurried, calculating days.
Arouse thee from thy reverie to view
The westering sun approach th' horizon dim
Of Marmora's blue wave ; thyself to find
A lone recluse among forget-me-nots
And frail anemonies, that rankly strew
The mouldering rampart of forsaken walls,
Which hear no sound except the sea-bird's scream,
And the incessant dash of restless waves
That murmuring die upon the shingly shore,
Or hurl the tempest-driven spray above
The parapet.   Majestic ships go by,
Their snowy pinions spread to every gale ;
Activity still flourishes among

Th' abodes of men ; but these old palaces
And crumbling towers forget the gladsome sound
Of pleasant footstep and of cheerful voice.

VIII.

Would'st stroll among Serai Bournû's[1] precincts ?
Approach with heart subdued the hallowed spot ;
Yes ! hallowed by associations sad.
Here thoughtful solitude reigns undisturbed :
The wild bird's song, heard seldom, strangely breaks
The solemn stillness, and the sun's bright warmth
Lies gloomy on the grassy terraces ;
The rose-tree and the weed together thrive,
In wild but sweet luxuriance, around
The moss-green sculptured fount, that jets no more
Its laughing stream.   The beauty lingering here
Is like the roseate glow on mountain peak,
When the sun's orb that lent that fervid hue
Has set behind the hills.   The bliss which rang
Whilome so blithely through these silent walks,
The souls whose life imparted life to these,
O, Spirit of the Past ! canst thou not tell
Where they are gone ? Perchance the vagrant shades
Of all the beautiful, the innocent,
The mighty and the brave, who loved this spot,
Long since returned to seek a covert lone
In these aged cypresses, that live and live,

---

[1] The Seraglio.

As Destiny had willed capriciously
That theirs be immortality's sweet boon.

The broken-hearted here may find a balm.
There is a soft, delicious sympathy
In the sad quietude which soothes the soul ;
And who is unacquainted with the pangs
Of preying sorrow ? — who that owneth not
Some little plot of earth that claims his sighs ?
The forlorn spirit, that holds fellowship
Unseen with forms evanished, oftentimes
In loneness feels a tender influence
Flattering its pains, which steals th' unbidden tear
From eyes that grief's intensity had dried,
And seems t' assuage the bitterness of woe ;
Then Sorrow cometh, veiled in twilight's hues,
A spirit celestial, and the prescient gaze
Imparts that sees into eternity.

And they whose noiseless ghosts here glide unseen,
Oft pleasure sowed but harvests rank to reap
Of sorrow, yea, of wild adversity !
The lily cheek, the sovereign's falcon eye,
The child, the sage, had each their turn to weep ;
And they were conscious, too, that dizzy life
Creeps on the margin of the sepulchre,
And planted long-lived trees in sombre groves,
Whose verdure rarely fades, to shield their tombs —
Affording shelter to the meek-eyed dove,
Whose plaintive moan should soothe their long repose.

IX.

Once on a time there lived an Emperor
Whose name was Valens.   Here he reigned, and oft
A Cæsar's pomp displayed along the streets
And sounding gateways of his capital.
At his command they reared an aqueduct;
And stone to stone, and lofty arch to arch
Were featly joined, each to its neighbor, till
There rose a stately edifice, that spanned
From hill to hill the space.   But now, of all
The multitudes who live and pass away
Within this fabric's mighty shadow, who
Has ever heard the perished name of Valens?
This pile stupendous testifies alone
To the forgotten fortunes of its liege.
The foliage springing from the gray cement
Flaunts through these arches to the morning sun,
And wavers in the moonbeams of the night,
Like funeral banners over coffined kings;
While down the furrowed stones the water drops
In tears of sorrow for a nation's woe.

X.

Behold where Sulymanié [1] looms up, —
A hoary, antiquated structure, — vast
But melancholy to the eye of him
Who stands observant of its awful dome.
Its sunlit windows seem like stars of eve

---

[1] The mosque of Sulymän.

In the vague, whisperous twilight that pervades
The cavernous vaults and carven galleries.
The timorous doves, which hover countlessly
In the chill, murmuring air from niche to niche
Among the sapphire pillars, as they would
From tree to tree in their green, native woods,
Methinks are symbols of the sacred peace
That mystically speaks in the deep echo
That rises from the hum of worshippers.

In the mosque court, in a secluded nook,
Two humble cupolas peep quietly
From out the coverture of slumberous boughs
Almost concealing them. The meagre wight
Who, shadow-like, dwells here, the devotee
Of a decaying creed, the stranger tells
That these are tombs. Oh, doubly happy he,
Who, coming to the end of life, shall find
So sweet a shelter for his mouldering dust!
Yes, Sulymân, the conqueror of men,
The Well-Beloved, long since to stern-browed Fate
Resigned the sceptre of extending power,
And, sore bewailed, was gathered to his fathers.

Within this sanctuary the hero lies ;
And Roxellana, she whose magic name
Thrilled sweeter than aught else upon his heart,
Wife of his bosom, in the other sleeps.
Dreamless repose ! pathetic solitude !

Where votive cypress, in its stillness weird,
Faithfully guards their everlasting slumber ;
While marigolds and fragrant wall-flowers bloom
So lonesomely around the sepulchres,
As if t' attract the cheerful sunlight here.
The passing traveller sometimes stops to gaze
On these abodes of fallen majesty,
Examining the shawls from far Cashmere
Which shroud the coffins, and the gems of price
That fitful glitter in the dusky light ;
And then as listlessly goes on his way,
And wots not of the tender tie that bound
Those throbless hearts, when life's emotions gushed
In their once swelling bosoms ; love so strong
That when the icy touch of Asrafel
Did silence them, the same mysterious trees
Should watch them laid in one beloved retreat ;—
Example strange of love, in age and clime
Sterile, alas ! in true connubial faith.

XI.

Behold the Hippodrome ! Wrapt Fancy's eye
Revives the racing steeds, the Greens, the Blues,[1]
The victors crowned with bay, the multitudes
Gazing impatient from the galleries,
The monarchs throned on high, the stately queens.
She hears once more glad music rise in swells
Of jubilant symphony, as cymbals clash

---

[1] Vide Gibbon's Rome, Chap. XI.

With lutes and mellow horns ; she hears again
The cries of faction drown the loudest strains
That metal breathes.   Time, passing here in haste,
Could not delay to gather all the spoil,
But, as the vintager in harvest leaves
Some purple clusters sparkling 'neath the vines,
The reaper of the world some gleanings left.

Here stands a cankered brazen pillar, formed
With triple convolutions serpentine ;
It came from bosky Delphi's sacred fane ;
Its serpents, headless now, once on their crests
Sustained the trophy of the Persian's fall.[1]
O, silver-voiced Hyperion ! — grant us yet
But one more oracle divine, to say
If this aged yet eternal capital,
This plaything of the nations, shall once more
Return unto the fickle Hellene's rule !
In vain ! — the Pythia is tuneless now !
At Liakûra's[2] foot the Delian's shrine
In ruin lies, obscurely desolate.
  *   *   *   *   *

XII.

Midnight th' imperial city wraps in gloom ;
Silence unbroken holds her solemn sway ;
Christian and Moslem, quick and dead, lie hushed,
Enwrapped in leaden Sleep's lethean pall.

---

[1] Xerxes.   [2] Mount Parnassus.

To thousands shall the morrow's sun renew
Life's strange vicissitudes. But many there
Nor morrow's sun, nor evening's starry host,
Nor flight of years, shall ever rouse again.
The clouds brood low, and there is music wild,
Sad music, on the housetops, as the wind
Whispers disconsolate, and nearer bears
The howling of the dogs that haunt the tombs,
And shadows steal along the dreary streets.
But, lo ! the sky glares ominously, as when
Autumnal mist droops o'er a mountain mere,
And through its veil the rising moon displays
A broad and crimson beacon on the hills.
The light grows brighter ; from afar a cry
Swells on the eddying breezes, — " Yangun Vâr !"[1]
Prolonged from house to house, from street to street,
The solemn warning thrills the hearer's soul,
Until the deep-mouthed cannon's sullen boom
Awakes the phantom echoes of Stambûl,
And bids her sleepers rise to grapple foes.

The sheeted flames roll onward ! — faster yet
The embers shoot ! Thus through th' eternal gloom
Of Polar skies the Sovran of the North
Showers his crackling arrows up the vault,
And robes his icy palaces with light.
Towering aloft in spectral majesty,
The minarets of many a sacred mosque

---

[1] There is fire — the appointed alarm-cry of the city.

Look from their lofty posts upon the scene,
As the tempestuous, fiery billows surge
With muttering thunders round the lurid heavens;
While piteous wretches gaze with streaming eyes
Upon the power whose rage devours their homes,
And wring their hands in unrestrained despair.

XIII.

Unhappy city! where the tooth of Time,
Forever gnawing at her holiest shrines,
Scarce executes the stern decrees of Fate,
Who frowns upon her beauty, and awaits
Impatient for her doom, — like fowl obscene
That ravens for its prey. She makes allies
The very elements, — the boisterous Waves,
That raze her battlements, — th' impetuous Fire,
That walks the streets by night, and publishes
With flaming tongues, to lands remote and wide,
The agonies of fallen Zaregrâd.[1]

Is this the city of whose regal pomps
Cathay heard, and the far isles of the sea,
And wondered at the tale? — the city clothed
With royalty, and decked with spoils of Ind?
Not such magnificence the elfin court
Of Oberon displayed in fairy-land;
Nor such the wealth Arabian poets sing
To have embellished Bagdad's fountained halls,
As rolling age on age was clustered round

---

[1] THE ROYAL CITY, as the Bulgarians call Constantinople.

The peerless rival of eternal Rome.
Superb with Tyrian purple sate her kings
Upon their golden thrones, nor dreamed of change :
Time came, beheld their pride, and where are they ?
The trumpet-blast of Islam's conquerors
Pealed o'er these domes : Time passed, looked on
      their pride,
And where are they ? — are they forever gone ?
So fades the sunset's pageantry of clouds !
When shall the humbled city rise again ?
When shall her desolation pass away ?
When shall she view reviving glory ? — when?
Even now the feeble remnant of her line
Is palsied by the finger of Despair :
Nemesis, wrapt in darkness, rides the storm,
And hurls abroad the thunderbolt of doom.
Hark ! on the toppling towers the Furies shriek !
I see their white hair streaming to the winds !
I hear their wild, blood-freezing howl of hate !

Weep, city of the Mighty Dead ! Oh, weep,
Offspring of wealth and valor ! Beauty's self !
A second Hero, by the seaside left
All desolate, to mourn thy sad estate ;
In vain thy cresset's blaze lights up the gloom,
To beacon to thine arms a race of kings.—
A glorious line, that shall no more return !
Let the soft harp-strings of the evening wind
Waft gently up to heaven thy sad laments,
And bid sweet Mercy turn and weep for thee !

THE ISLE OF PEARLS.

THE ISLE OF PEARLS.

Soft plays the tide along the shore,
  Soft sighs the zephyr on the sea,
Soft dips the fisher's silver oar —
  All sounds make pleasant harmony.
Above th' horizon's distant rim
  The moon is seen, like midnight ghost,
And o'er the deep her glances gleam,
  And whiten all the lonely coast.
A bark rides in the solemn bay,
  Her silken pinions woo the breeze,
Her sheeny prow is wet with spray,
  And pointed to the southern seas.
How beautiful your shadows seem,
  O sea, O shore, O gilded bark,
As, gliding through my passing dream,
  Ye bid my ear entrancéd hark
To the wild notes that float away
From the fair bark that rides the bay!

"O thou, that wanderest on the strand,
 Gazing upon the heaving swell,
Why tarry longer on the land? —
 To shore and mountain say farewell,
And, to the melody of song,
 And murmur of sweet-sighing sails,
In this brave galley sweep along
 Before the soft and favoring gales.
Away. away, beyond the sea,
 Behold the star-bespangled halls,
Where souls in harmony agree,
 And the foam sheaf of fountains falls
From night to day, from day to night,
 Throughout the ages as they go,
While birds do ever wing their flight
 Above the floods that brimming flow,
And roseate pearls and lamps illume
 The bowers that by the ocean smile,
And twinkle through the scented gloom
 That cools the palace of the isle.
Then come away, O lingering soul,
 Then take thy midnight flight with me,
Where the wild waves more peaceful roll,
 And the lone islet gilds the sea."

I listened to the luring maid,
 Who on the awned poop did sing.
The while her veil in dalliance played
 Unto her witching caroling:

Enraptured then, I leaped aboard
  A shallop fastened to the shore,
And swiftly to the galley oared,
  That straightway ceased in port to moor ;
The sails were trimmed by hands unseen ;
  We left behind a gleaming wake,
That, as we skimmed the waters green,
  Broke round the keel in many a flake.
The music of Eolian wires
  The lonely voyage did beguile,
Until the morrow's sunset fires
  Revealed the palace of the isle.
The sun went down ; up rose the moon ;
  Rustled the shadowy groves of palm
Unto a low and measured tune,
  That whispered of eternal calm.
In the white light pavilions shone,
  With fluted pillars all arow,
Reminding of the times agone,
  And mirrored in the depths below ;
The sound of waterfalls was heard
  From sheltered vales and sparry caves,
And the long trill of twilight's bird
  Chimed with the drone of plunging waves
Trees, hoary with the vapory spume,
  Around the dreamy porches hung,
Diffusing shade and mild perfume
  Like odorous incense censer-flung :

Light such as one beholds in dreams
    Floated o'er all the sea-girt spires,
While, flitting in the spectral beams,
    Their plumage waved seraphic quires,
And hymned forevermore a song
That breathed the death of sin and wrong,
And the mild reign of soothing peace,
And virtue that should never cease;
    And mellow-tunéd virginals
Were struck by elves, who tripped in rows
    Fantastic measures through the halls,
With garlands woven round their brows:
    The ocean lapped the stairs of marble,
That green with agéd mosses were,
    As, by their music's amorous warble
Attracted in, I landed there.
    A diadem of pearls was hung
Down from the midst o' the centre dome,
    And round it were these accents sung
By a fair group, all mirth and bloom.

"What are days and months and years,
    What is age and what is time,
Unto those who shed no tears,
    And behold no grief or crime?
For we mark the fleeting hours
By the blooming of the flowers
Which are nursed in amaranthine bowers.

" Round these arches high festoon
    Wreaths of lilies dropped with dew ;
Ope the lattice — let the moon
    Stream its wizard radiance through,
Stealing o'er mosaic floors,
While we dance away the hours
In the shadow of enchanted towers.

" Hangs upon the string a pearl
    For each one of us that sings ; —
Sorrow shall her pinions furl,
    Glad shall sound our murmurings,
And those pearls like stars shall shine,
While unitedly we join
In the strain of melodies divine.

" Concord rules the Sacred Seven,
    Tuning all the starry throng ;
Harmony is found in heaven,
    Angel's theme and seraph's song.
Guardian of the chiming spheres,
Listen to our sister prayers,
And preserve our isle from sorrow's cares.

" For if sorrow enter here,
    Yonder pearls would soon grow dim ;
These arcades would disappear ;
    Hushed would be our evening hymn.

Then, sweet Spirit of the spheres,
Listen to our sister prayers,
And preserve our isle from sorrow's cares."

———————

The strain through arc and oriel
    In breezy whispers kissed the deep;
The halcyon floating on the swell
    Woke raptured from her midnight sleep;
And in the emerald depths profound
The mermaids heard the eddying sound.

II.

Methought a change passed through my dream :
    A grisly shape, with raven plume,
Perched on a pinnacle did seem
    Like owlet on an ancient tomb ;
The diadem began to fade,
    The singer's music ceased to flow,
The moon's soft splendor grew more sad,
    And over all a " nameless woe "—
Mute desolation's silent spell —
Spread like a mourner's sable veil.
Fair as the clustering Pleiades,
    Linked hand in hand, the sister's stood
Upon the airy terraces
    That overarchedthe solemn flood.

But one, the queenliest of the band,
To seaward waved her ivory hand,
Standing apart, nigh to the edge
Of the high gallery's outer ledge.
Pale jessamine her dainty wrists
    And flowing tresses garlanded ;
Her vesture clasped her form as mists
    Clothe pensive Morning's radiant head.
Majestic grace was on her brow —
    She seemed in act to mount above —
Yet throbbed her bosom with the glow
    Of woman's deep, undying love.
Pure-eyed she was — one that would die
For him who claimed her fondest sigh.

By this the moon hung very low ;
    And o'er the waters dark and lone
The night wind wailed a sound of woe,
    And the stars, one by one, went down.
" Last night he called — this night he calls,"
    The Nereid to her sisters spake ;
" I must forsake my native halls,
    Before the glimmering morning break.
O love ! I list his murmuring shell —
    I can no longer tarry here :
Farewell, sweet sisters, fare ye well !
    Why shed the unavailing tear ?
Why should your guileless bosoms mourn ?
Shall I not hither soon return ?

Enchanter of the mystic sea !
I faint with love — I come to thee ! "
The maiden wrapped her white cymar
   More close around her limbs of snow,
Then dropping like a falling star,
   Plunged in the moaning flood below.
In vain the sisters, all forlorn,
   Upon the rivage watched the main,
If haply with some rising morn
   The lost one should return again.
The elfish cressets lit no more
The fairy palace on the shore ;
Nor did the pearly diadem
At any time its radiance beam.
The dusky bird, that Woe was hight,
   Forevermore its station kept,
And through each long, long, lingering night
   The statue-fountains ceaseless wept.
The flocks, that tender grasses nibbled
   Upon the island's pastoral swells,
No longer browsed where runnels dribbled,
   Nor shook at dusk their rural bells ;
For they who wont to feed their lambs,
   And drive them forth at dewy dawn,
Or lead them 'neath umbrageous palms
   At highest noon, were now forlorn,
Weeping beside the sounding sea
For their lost queen incessantly —
The shepherdess whose gentle soul

Delighted in the lambkin's bleat ;
The virgin fair who nightly stole
   O'er paven floors with nimble feet,
And in the blaze of flashing torches
Attuned soft strains through echoing porches.
But ne'er again the Nereid came,
Nor with the morn or sunset flame.

Then on the bark that brought me there
I stepped aboard ; the gale was fair ;
And soon below the ocean's blue
The lonely isle was lost to view.

3

THE SAILOR-BOY.

THE SAILOR-BOY.

'T WAS Autumn. By the lane the farm-house stood,
Th' abode of peace and plenty. Slowly curled
The smoke above the chimney, purple wreaths
Illumined by the sunset, and the cock
Crew in the barnyard all the livelong hours.
Before the door the farmer's daughter trained
The clambering honeysuckle, and the while
Murmured a simple ditty wild with love.
Her urchin brothers gambolled by the brook
That warbled through the wood and down the lane :
This launched his tiny boat upon the stream,
Those built a mimic dam, and shouted loud
With childish glee. The jocund watch-dog bayed
Unto the flying echoes, and the crow
Flapped dreamy pinions in the stilly air.
Dim through the thin and melancholy mist
Of Indian Summer rose the russet hills,
And on the village spire, a far-off flame,
The vane gleamed like a solitary star.
But, hark ! upon the yellow leaves that strew

The shady path, a faltering step is heard.
A youth is seen approaching, on his staff
Leaning most wearily.　His tattered garb
Scarce hides his wasted form ; and what a tale
Of sore distress his sunken eye, wan cheek,
And bloodless lip declare !　The lads forsake
Their noisy sport, abashed, as they behold
A stranger ; and old Rover wistful looks
Into the wanderer's face, who now has reached
The quiet homestead.　" Give me but a crust,
A meagre crust, sweet maiden ; I am faint,"
He said unto the damsel by the door,
And then sank down upon the mossy trunk
Of a long-fallen oak, oppressed with pain.
Quickly her gentle eye discerned the woe
Which mastered him, and, with a voice that broke
Upon his ear like moonlight on the sea,
When it is troubled by tumultuous winds,
She answered : " Enter ; rest thee, traveller ; — soon
From pasture will the kine return, and then
The foaming milk, warm in the brimming bowl,
Thy vigor shalt restore."　His following eye
Spake gratitude, when, seated 'neath the roof,
Beside the blazing hearth, he watched the grace
With which the farmer's daughter blessed her home.

" Tarry with us this night ; the morrow morn
Depart refreshed," the hale old farmer said.
Therefore he tarried, and beguiled the hours

Of the long autumn evening with the tale
Of his late woes and wanderings.   Thus it ran :

" Fair blew the breezes when we sailed from port.
Day after day our clipper southward sped,
For we were bound unto the land of gold.
Six nights we ploughed the main ; the seventh brought
Thick darkness o'er the deep.   Then shrieked the gale
Through straining cordage, and the rent sails flapped
Like demons' pinions in the murky gloom.
From billow on to billow plunged the prow ;
And in the midst we heard the cry of fire.
Forth from the hatches burst the stifling smoke ;
The wild winds breathed with fury on the flames ;
The embers flew across the reeling deck, —
A crackling shower, — and the thundering fires
Leaped up the tapering masts, and licked the sails
From the slant yards, and kissed the driving clouds.
The Captain shouted : " To the boats ! " in haste
We launched away ; the longboat and the yawl,
Upon the stormy waters tossing, bore
Twelve souls, to fearful thirst and famine doomed.
Before us drove our bark ; athwart her sides
The furnace glowed ; her ribs were ribs of fire.
The tempest tossed the burning ropes aloft
Like fiery serpents, and the maddened surge
That lashed her noble prow, was all aflame
Beneath that ruddy blaze — the sheeted foam
Was like to foam of blood.   Far o'er the sea

The supernatural glare made midnight's gloom
More horrible.   But suddenly it paled,
And then went out in darkness.   On the waves
We drifted till the cold, gray dawn arrived.
But when the morning broke, my shipmates peered
Through the salt mist of driving spray, with eyes
Made keen by fierce despair, but spied in vain.
No comrade boat was visible ; alone
We rode the sad, interminable waste
Of ocean; land, nor sail, nor sun, in sight.
The billows snapped our oars ; we had no mast ;
We were the playthings of the storm, and sat
Upon the crazy thwarts disconsolate,
Wan-featured, hopeless, save that each did hope
The bitter pleasure of first hailing death.

" Three days we buffeted the hurricane,
And toiled with failing strength to keep afloat,
Shifting from side to side, as hung the surge
Impending o'er the gunwale ; but the fourth
Came, ushering calms, and burning heat, and thirst.
That quickly drained our water's scanty store.
The seventh day, at dawn, a gray-haired man
Drew a long sigh and died.   With trembling hands
We gave the carcass to the deep, but shed
No pitying tears ; for each did envy him
His timely fate.   The eighth sad dawn revealed
Two stark and rigid corpses in the boat ;
Their fixed, glazed eyeballs glared so fearfully

Upon us, that we shuddered as with cold,
Although the sun's fierce ardor showered heat
Over the simmering sea.   We quailed beneath
The dead men's gaze ; therefore we mustered strength
To heave them overboard.   But two were left.
My comrade perched himself upon the bow ;
I sat me in the stern.   The day wore on ; —
We dozed and dreamed wild dreams ; — we syllabled
Strange, incoherent ravings ; but we dared
Not glance into each other's eye ; — each feared
That he might soon be food to satisfy
His neighbor's cravings, and we groaned aloud.

" That evening, as the crimson moon drew nigh
The ocean, dashing o'er the shifting waves
A spectral gleam, and on my comrade's face
A ghastly hue, I heard a sudden plunge, —
I looked, and he was gone !   Perchance a fit
Had stiffened his weak frame ; perchance despair
Had urged him to his doom.   I spied a shark,
With hungry maw, slide all his fearful length
Through the green water, by the tossing boat,
Where moon-lit bubbles showed the corpse had sunk ;
And then I thanked my God, who saved his child
From the dark sin of tasting human flesh.

" Vanished the moon.   The ripples lapped the boat,
Which wandered solitary on the sea.

I heard the low, shrill winds, in dreary sobs,
Ruffling the tranquil ocean all that night,
That dreadful night, when I was all alone ; —
Yet not alone.   Around me in the air
Weird voices whispered ; and where he had sat,
My latest shipmate, now I saw a shape
Of spectral whiteness, skeleton of form,
And gazing steadfastly through me with eyes
That curdled all my blood with their fixed spell ;
The while the apparition seemed to say,
' Thou, too, art mine !'   I was alone with Death !
The pangs of hunger, which had gnawed my flesh,
Were then as naught beside the terrible dreams
That in the wild, appalling solitude
Haunted and tortured me.   I fled along
The margin of a precipice.   Above
Beetled an adamantine wall ; beneath
There plunged a bottomless abyss, from whence
Arose the wailing cries of dying souls ;
And ever as I ran that giddy race
A spectre dogged my steps.   Eternity
Seemed all too short to fly the fearful fiend !
He stretched his arm to clutch my hair, — I shrieked,
And, shrieking, woke ; but woke to see those eyes,
Those dreadful eyes, turned steadily on mine ; —
Those bloody eyes, whose serpent gaze is burned
With such intensity upon my brain,
That to this day their memory thrills my soul.

" I dreamed and woke alternately, and thus
That night of agony wore on.   At last
The morning broke, and brought my spirit peace.
The wind had wafted south the drifting boat,
And to the leeward lay an Indian isle.
Then, as I floated shoreward, on the ridge
Of craggy mountains I discerned the groves
Of cocoa pencilled 'gainst the sky,
And saw the thin, blue spires of smoke ascend
Above the tree-tops, where the islanders
Nestled in wattled huts among the woods.
A bird flew off from land, and hovered round
My tempest-beaten head, and perched itself
Upon the boat-side, pouring forth such strains
Of rapturous melody from its glad throat
That brimming tears suffused my parchéd eyes.
They saw me not on shore, or, if they saw,
Thought me, perchance, a fisher of their tribe;
And thus, when evening came, and up the vault
The sun shot rosy gleams before he sank
Behind the slender palms, the veering wind
Blew gently off the bay, and bore my skiff
Again to sea.   Soft, odorous balms were blown
On the mild breeze, and, in the dewy dusk,
The island's star-like torches twinkled o'er
The peaceful water.   Then I might have wept
To leave so fair a prospect, which allured
My desolate soul with beauty as of Eden ;
But in my troubled bosom now there reigned

A settled calm ; too weak was I to rave ;
I felt resigned to my approaching fate.
But now, where Death had kept his watch abhorred,
A seraph lighted, waving golden plumes,
As if to pilot me to that unknown,
Mysterious sea to which we all are bound.
Above me, in the firmament serene,
The Southern Cross with marvellous splendor shone,
Symbol of Him who died upon the tree :
And as I watched that night the wondrous sign,
Awe, blent with fervent love, o'erpowered my soul,
Until sweet slumber kissed my wearied lids.

" I saw again in dreams my boyhood's home, —
The gambrel cottage, with its quaint old roof,
Beneath whose mossy eaves the swallows sang ;
Over the chimney waved the weeping elm
To the low west wind ; in the cornfields gleamed
The golden maize — the farmer's joy ; near by
Murmured the grove of pines, with bickering brooks
Gambolling around the rugged roots, and forth
Into the meadow stealing.   In the fields,
And up the hollow by the river, rang
The voices of haymakers, and the air
Wafted the fragrance of the tedded grass.
And then I wandered to the well, and slaked
My thirst out of the bucket round whose brim
Sparkled the gushing dew ; and as I drank,
Behold, reflected in the well, a face,

And when I looked, lo! at my side she stood —
The sister of my boyhood, golden-haired,
With eyes that spake to me of heaven.   My sweet,
My own sweet sister Alice! thou hast lain
In the cold graveyard winters four; yet then
Thou didst return and bless me with thy love,
As in my childhood.   When I sailed alone
In unimaginable solitude
Upon the solemn, melancholy sea,
Thy voice was music to my fainting soul!
Before the open window she, so long
Father and mother to me, sat and read
In her ancestral Bible of that world
Whose glories were reflected on her brow.

" But all things had a vague, unearthly hue;
I knew 't was but a dream within a dream.
Even the magic rustle of the leaves
Now seemed like phantom echoes wafted down
From nations sepulchred in dust and gloom
Centuries ago.   And then my vision changed.
I heard the peal of lordly music roll
Over an eastern landscape; and I saw
A stately host, with royalty and pomp,
Magnificently marching, days and days,
Unto a rampired city far away
In the sand desert; but when they had gained
The open gates the habitants had fled
Their capital, and all the wells were dry.

And thus the wretches, overcome by thirst,
Crowded around the fountains that gave forth
No water, looked to heaven, and, gasping, died.
In the lone streets their whitened bones were strown,
And vultures garrisoned the battlements.

" The thought of that parched multitude renewed
Th' intolerable thirst that burned my tongue,
And fevered all my brain with agony,
Which, as I woke, convulsed my shrivelled frame
With such stern anguish that mortality
Seemed loosening her bonds.   At that dark hour, —
That moment fraught with death, — my sinking eye
Beheld a sail ! — a sail ! it was a sail,
A real vessel, skimming o'er the waves !
Oh ! in my sailor wanderings I have seen
Full many a noble spectacle ; but when
My raptured vision fell upon that ship,
And saw her masts aspiring to the skies,
Her royals purpled by the radiant flush
That heralded the yet unrisen sun,
Her courses swelling to the morning breeze,
The foam-flakes wreathing round her keen, sharp
        prow,
And majesty and beauty in her shape,
As, with a swan-like motion, o'er the sea
She glided ; then I thought that human eye
Had never rested on a sight more fair,
More noble, than that bark which brought me life.

" With ecstasy I leaped up in the boat,
But in a swoon fell back. I knew no more
Until my hot, sere eyeballs were unsealed
To gaze on pitying eyes, and see a form
Of angel loveliness beside my couch,
With cooling drink and words that murmured peace.
Slowly my strength returned; and when we reached
The destined port, I crept on deck to view
The looming harbor. To the wharves we moored,
And then the hospital became my home :
And there I lingered till they said to me
' Go — let another take thy bed.' I went,
Knowing too well that but a short reprieve
Was granted me of life; and then I thought,
' My voyage is almost o'er — the haven's near
In which my shattered hulk shall moor forever;
Therefore I 'll seek my boyhood's roof, and die
With my dear mother's hand upon my brow.'
And thither now I journey; but methinks
I ne'er shall reach it more. My tale is done.
But when the wild winds howl aloof, then pray
For the poor mariner who roams the sea,
And climbs the slippery mast, and hears the peal
Of midnight thunder shake his tossing bark."

And yet the tale was not all told. That night
Death came, not on the solitary deep,
But in the moonlit chamber where the youth
Had laid him down to slumber. Death was now

No spectre, but an angel bringing sleep.
And the youth slept; and when the swallow hailed
The morrow morn, nor waked the sailor-boy,
The kindly farmer sought the sleeper's room,
And found him dead.   A placid beauty veiled
The sunken features, and his silken hair
Curled on the marble brow most tenderly.
With many tears the gathering villagers
Buried the stranger in the silent grave,
And marked it with a slab, and wrote thereon,
"SWEET TO THE WEARY MARINER IS REST."

ERIC AND EDITH;

A TALE OF THE NORTH.

ERIC AND EDITH;

A TALE OF THE NORTH.

THERE was high wassail in the Norseman town:
The daring corsairs of the foaming seas
Had moored their barks once more within the port
From whence they hailed, and all their kith and clan
Now welcomed them with boisterous mirth. Loud rang
The berserk's song; wild were the tales they told,
As maidens passed the mead, and eagle eyes
Did sparkle o'er the sparkling beaker's brim.

But Eric, by the revelers unobserved,
Stole to the castle turret, there to find
His Edith waiting for her love. Two years
Had lent her flaxen locks a darker hue,
And to her form imparted riper grace; —
Two years had lit his eye with nobler fire,
With manlier thew and sinew knit his frame,
Since last they met. Their eyes spake welcome sweet,
Spake words of rapture, which their speechless lips

Essayed not.   Thus the moments sped, until
The moon loomed o'er the northern sea, and beamed
Her holy benison upon their vows.
Then Eric's heart found utterance in this wise :

"My Edith, when I told thee of my love,
These many moons ago, thou didst confess
The warmth of thy affection, saying still,
' And if indeed thou lov'st me, let me have
A token that thy heart is true.   Unfurl
Thy galley's idle sails, and southward steer,
Where lie those gorgeous lands of which they tell
Such wondrous legends.   Be a hero now ; —
Not only for the glory of thy name,
But for the love thou bear'st to Edith, brave
And overcome new perils.'   I have been.
Yes, where the citron's golden fruitage breathes
Its languid odors over sapphire seas ;
Where olive-skirted hamlets seem to hang
In air high up the mountain sides ; where towers,
White in the sun, crown every cape, and speak
Of long-departed power ; where vineyards clothe
The various landscape, — there the Viking's keel
Adventurous has glided.   There, at dead
Of night, I've landed on th' unguarded coast,
And stormed the Southron's hold, and borne away
Unnumbered spoils or ever dawn appeared.
And there, in Rome's imperial capital,
I climbed prodigious ruins, and did hear

In the mysterious twilight awful sounds,
The din of vanished generations, like
The roar of distant tempests through the pines
Of Norway's forests. But a soft, low voice
Came murmuring to my ear, that said, ' My love,
Come home, come home!' Then, with exulting soul,
I shouted, ' Northward turn the iron beak
Of the War Eagle, for our cruise is done!'
And when the storm-winds rose in wrath to check
Our homeward course, and swept the deck with sleet
And foam, — when in the blackening midnight quailed
The stoutest heart, — I saw thy chosen star,
The polar star, gleam through the driving scud,
And kiss the angry waves with argent beam ; —
The thought of thee rekindled hope ; I grasped
The rudder, and we rode the blast unharmed.
And when we neared Scandinia's misty coast,
Two many-bucklered prores bore down. Thy love
Gave vigor to my arm; and this we sunk,
With all her bearded crew, and that I brought
To port, a token of my love. Lo ! where
She lies in yonder haven, black-hulled and huge
In the broad moon's white shadow. And behold
These clustering pearls, a queenly diadem,
Another token of my passion, gained
What time I gained this scar. But what are all
Affection's tributes worth if once compared
With th' undivided offering of the heart —
The true heart of a hero ? — Such I gave

My Edith long ago. And now what more
Desires my dove, the darling of my soul?"

The maiden gazed into the warrior's face
With look of love, and pride, and gratitude,
Yet mingled with a vague, unsatisfied
Expression in her eye. At length she said:
"Thou know'st I love thee, and I trust thy faith,
Thou noble heart and true; and still before
I yield myself to thee a willing slave,
I fain would prove thee further; 't is a freak —
A foolish maiden's freak — but yet a freak
I cherish. Thou hast vowed that thou wouldst die
If love should doom thee so. And now I pray
This boon: — Explore the ocean bound with ice,
A thousand leagues away, and bring me thence
A robe of fur, the silver fox's dower
Unto thy bride. My heart shall speed thy prow,
And when thou art returned, then call me thine."

Days passed, and Eric, beautiful as Balder,
Strode on his deck and mustered all his crew
Of grim marauders, gave his swelling sheet
Unto the winds, and sailed into the North.

The slow moons waxed and waned, until the light
Of a full score had faded from the skies,
Nor did the long-departed bark return;

And when Norwegian galleys made the port
From time to time, men, women, children, flocked
Along the strand to meet the voyagers,
Demanding loudly, " Have ye nowhere seen
The Day Star of the North upon the seas,
Adventurous Eric ?   Have ye nowhere hailed
The proud War Eagle on the mighty main,
Snorting the foam-flakes from her iron prow ? "
And all with one accord replied, " Nowhere,
Nor in the south, nor in the far-off waste
Of waves, where bathes the sun his burning brow,
Nor in the north, have we beheld the hero."
And there was grief, heart-breaking grief, I ween,
In the dun tower that watched the roaring sea.
Through the long nights, that grew more long, until
Unbroken night seemed hovering o'er her soul,
Edith her vigils kept, and trimmed her lamp
To guide the wanderer home.   Why did he tarry ?
Alas for swan-necked Edith !   Knew he not
That her soft eye was red with tears ? — that love
For him, and expectation unfulfilled,
Had stolen the blush of gladness from her cheek ?
Alas for Edith ! — why did Eric tarry?

But when the third sweet springtime had returned,
And loosed the waters of the northern meres,
And breathed its magic through the forest firs,
Then Harold, chieftain of the flowing hair,
Brother to Edith, said : " My sister, cease

Thy wailing; for the love I bear to thee,
And for that I remember me of all
The scenes of happiness that we enjoyed
In childhood's days together, and because
Thy Eric was my friend, I'll launch my keel,
And search the ice-bound sea until I find,
And to thy heart restore, the long-lost lover.
Now, therefore, sweet my sister, weep no more."

Again a year passed by; and then it chanced
Upon an evening when the clouds grew black
Above the ocean, and the white seamews
'Gan prophesy a storm, and all the ships
Were safely moored ashore, there sped a youth
Into the town with tidings. "Norsemen, ho!
Harold the yellow-haired has come — is here!"
Thence to the castle straight the stripling ran
Wide-mouthed, loud-heralding to all he met,
"Harold the yellow-haired has come — is here!"

That night a storm swept o'er those northern lands,
Such as the oldest there had never known;
But in the castle hall nor boom of surf
Nor thundering winds were heeded. Round the fire
The Norsemen gathered, while the crackling flames
Roared up the chimney, casting elfish gleams
Over grim features rough from fight and storm;
And with his vassals sat the aged Jarl,

In the accustomed corner, and he quaffed
The foaming mead, and stroked his snowy beard,
And gazed with pride upon his first-born — Harold;
While Edith sat, with eyes bedimmed by tears,
Between her brother and her sire.   And then
Did Harold thus rehearse his mournful tale.

"Northwest we sailed for many days.   Thick clouds
And dripping mist o'er-canopied our bark,
And the keen air grew colder evermore.
Nor moon nor stars were seen.   Once, at high noon,
The sun, well-nigh eclipsed, was dim descried —
A ball of copper driving through the scud.
At length the fog-clouds fled, and far away
All the blue offing gleamed with glittering spires,
As if the serried spears of some great host
Had caught the glory of the rising day;
We saw the region of perpetual ice.
With hearts undaunted, we advanced to meet
The mighty multitude of bergs.   At even
We sailed into the solemn capital
Where reigns alone the Monarch of the North.
Awe-struck and dumb with wonder, we were borne
Through sinuous channels, where the heaving flood
Rolled darkly in the gloom of palaces
Hewn out of ice from immemorial years.
The full-orbed moon sheened all the pinnacles
With unimaginable splendor, while
The twinkling stars engrailed the liquid streets

With arrowy shafts of silver.　But no sound
Of living habitant was heard throughout
That city vast.　Mysterious silence, grim,
Supernal, hovered there.　The distant boom
Of the dull surge, the sea-bird's fitful scream,
The murmurous dash of runnels dribbling down
The icy cliffs and chasms — these were not sounds —
They were but whispers faintly breathed to him
Who slumbers; we were like to one awake
At midnight, listening, with a panting heart,
To the weird voice of Silence.　Then the wind
With spirit sobbings left us, and with sweeps
Or grapples closely clasping crystal wharves,
We traversed the canals, and neared broad fields
Of ice interminable, here and there
Thridded by creeks of water dark as lead,
Through which our galley glided, compassed round
With thickening perils, as the floating slabs
Of jagged ice against the iron prow
Did harshly grate, or o'er the bulwarks tower.

"Thus northward held our course, until we dared
No further venture, but our longing sight
Had yet no Eric found.　The summer months
Were failing fast — fast fled the genial days;
The birds flew southward, and the time had come
Which bade us follow their unswerving flight,
Ere winter should imprison us forever.
In vain had been each anxious search, or where

The iceberg soared in majesty asky,
Or where the cairn revealed its dim recess,
Or where tumultuous piles of hummocks rose
Like heaps of ruins.   Not a single trace
Of man or bark was yet discovered there.
Not even a shattered spar on which to hang
The sign of Hope.   The bleak autumnal winds
Whistled more wildly o'er those sterile fields
Of ice eternal, and we heard our wives
And children call us to our blazing hearths.
And then we said, 'Let one last search be made
Before we sail.'   I led my comrades on.
Two days we journeyed, till at set of sun,
Far down in the horizon, like a cloud
Of thinnest violet, we saw a peak
Aspiring to the stars.   That night the skies
Were crimsoned with a glory like the glare
Of a vast conflagration; waves of red
Swept zenithwards like lightning; all the bergs
Were robed with purple, and their brows were crowned
With living rubies, and the welkin rang
With strange, mysterious noises.   By that light
We travelled through the watches of the night,
But found no Eric.   Underneath the peak
Of which I spake we halted, and, despair
Within our hearts, held council to return.

"At that last moment I did climb a cliff
That overlooked the whole surrounding space,

And glanced below.   There, in a tomb of ice,
The dear old ship, the stout, the brave War Eagle,
Had found her grave !   The mast was upright still,
But from the swinging yard the tattered sail
Had parted long ago.   The ice hung high
Above the gunwale, threatening instant wreck,
Yet motionless, save when th' explosive shock
From distant floes thrilled through the glittering mass.
Eric the chieftain sat him on the poop,
With all his faithful Norsemen ranged around.
A ghastly group it was — their bare ribs mailed
With hauberks, and their skulls yclad with helms ;
Full five and twenty skeletons were there,
All stiff and silent, and we knew each one
From the worn scutcheon on his battered shield ;
But Eric had enshrouded his gaunt form
In a long robe of silver foxes' skins.
Brave spirit ! he had fought in many a fight,
And overcome full many a foe ; but when
He grasped his mighty brand for the last time,
He lost the victory, for he fought with Death !

" Oh, when I stood beside that fleshless frame,
That in its silence seemed so eloquent,
And called to mind the times when we had slept
Like brothers, by the same fur mantle wrapt,
Beneath the winter starlight, when we chased
The surly bear across the frozen lakes ; —
Oh, when I thought of that great heart now chill

Within his icy bosom, — that stout heart
Which oftentimes had nerved his good right arm
To battle valiantly, — that heart which loved
As never woman loved, — then was my breast
Convulsed with sorrow, and I wept — even I,
A warrior Viking, wept — as I do now !
Strike all your harps, ye Skalds, and let your shells
Sweep solemn dirges for the fallen brave !
Lift up your voices in th' ancestral halls,
And chant his glory in immortal runes ! "

Here ceased the tale, and silence for a space
Held all the listeners. Louder pealed the storm,
Shaking the rugged bawn's embattled towers ;
But when it lulled, and in the distance wailed,
A long-drawn sigh was heard, scarce audible,
Yet full of agony, and Edith's head
Upon her father's bosom lifeless fell.

THE BRIDE OF BRUSA.

THE BRIDE OF BRUSA.

With silly noise, the sleepy crow,
Perching on yonder leafless bough
   Upon the cliff's apex,
   The dreamy stillness breaks :
The white clouds of an April day
Hang o'er the mountain tops full low :
The traveller, on his dappled-gray,
Along the gorge pursues his lonely way.

The bearded monk, the anchorite,
With russet garb and locks of white,
   Suns him before his cave,
   A little warmth to save
For him decrepit, while he saith,
As ever doing morn and night
With fervor and unceasing breath,
His paters on the rosary of his faith.

" Friend hermit," quoth the traveller,
" Perchance canst tell, lone caloyer,[1]

---

[1] Monk.

Wherefore, on rocky ledge,
　Yon tower, begrimmed with age,
And draped all o'er with ivy green,
Deserted stands of dwellers there;
　Why sentinel of warlike mien
No more upon its battlements is seen?"

"Ah me! too curious, thou wouldst know
　A tragedy replete with woe.
　　It was a chieftain bold,
　　Who lived in days of old,
　That built those turrets dark and high,
　Some eighty waning years ago.
　Long moons the watchsound might'st descry
Alternate with the poising eagle's cry.

"He was a chieftain known to fame,
　And Kara Yani was his name ;
　　But though of sturdy heart,
　　With many a kindly art
　He offered shelter unto me,
　When to the castle gate I came :
　I was content for him to be
A beadsman, and for his wild soldiery.

"Adventurous mountaineers were they
　Who there maintained a petty sway;
　　And oft, with spoil and slave,
　　With recking lance and glaive,

Like lions to their desert lair,
They strode along the winding way
Unto the fortress ; then the air
Of night was lit up by the torch's flare :

" When, resting from the midday's toils,
  The victors counted o'er their spoils,
      While glittern's ceaseless thrumming,
      And love-song's plaintive humming,
  Attuned the watches of the night.
  Alas ! grim age my memory foils
  About those times when yon dark height
Was brightened by the wassail's fitful light.

" The chieftain's daughter, full of grace,
  Did flourish in that barren place
      Like flower that scents the air
      On precipices bare ;
  And one might see a passing gleam
  Upon the soldier's rugged face,
  Chance, too, a tear his eye would dim,
What time the maiden lisped her simple hymn.

" Oh, she was fair in opening bloom,
  That bud which cheered our castle home !
      Her eyes were smiling blue,
      Like turtle's, mild of hue ;
  Her golden ringlets, flowing down,
  Were soft as silk from Brusa's loom ;

Her sportiveness and beauty won
Upon my heart, as if she were my own.

" I bore her oft the hills among, —
    For then these arms were young and strong, —
        Where she could hear the quail
        Along the heathery vale,
    Or sweet bulbûl by shady stream ;
 . I taught her many a holy song,
    And hung her neck with cross that came
From sacred olive in Jerusalem.

" She had a glister-eyed gazelle, —
    A frisky thing she cherished well, —
        Which loved to wander aye
        Where'er the maid did stray ;
    And oft her voice rang through the tower
    Symphonious with her pet's sweet bell.
    She loved to train the blushing flower,
And cull spice-scented basil evermore.

" While yet a boy of tender age,
    Before I went on pilgrimage,
        There was an airy form,
        With playful ardor warm,
    Who wont to call me brother dear,
    As soft her arms my neck did cage
    With fond caress, and lulled my ear
Ofttimes with childish prattle sweet to hear.

" But 't was full many a weary year
   Since I had heard her accents clear;
      Since last so tenderly
      My little sister's eye
   Beamed on me with her young heart's love;
   Then was it strange, O traveller!
   That when I ceased the earth to rove,
I doted on the chieftain's little dove?

" But when to bashful maidenhood,
   Gently as bow looms on the cloud,
      She glided softly then,
      The lovely, fair Elene,
   A damsel coy, she needs must hide
   Within the lattice-gloomed abode;
   And there she passed her summer tide,
Until a hero sought her for his bride.

" The lord of Biledjik's domain,
   He stole, with love's bewitching chain,
      The singing bird that blest
      Her native mountain nest:
   Ah, woful time, when evermore
   They taught her hidden to remain!
   But still more sad the fatal hour
When she forsook her father's stately door.

" For many days the festival
   They kept, with dance and atabal;

Our youth, on flying steeds,
Tilted with quivering reeds;
Their clatter rang for noondays nine
Around the castle's lofty wall;
And eyes that flashed like Sciote wine
There were, but none, Elene, so bright as thine!

" It was the spicy month of June;
And nightly rose the silent moon,
And with a silver shower
Illumined vale and tower.
The nightingale we heard, between
The bursts of song, trill out her tune, —
A fitting harmony, I ween,
For happier, merrier bridal ne'er was seen.

" And so the joyful season flew;
But, ah! Osmân, the caitiff, knew
That Biledjik was lone,
With paltry garrison.
Then flashed his eye with pride and hate;
His jewel-hilted blade he drew,
Waved it aloft, and cried, elate,
' Mine, mine is Biledjik! 't is doomed by Fate!'

" You still might see the star of morn
Gleam through the golden edge of dawn;
The fog lay white and dank
Amid the rushes rank

That fringe the streamlet's oozy brink;
And timidly the meek-eyed fawn
Came sauntering down for woodland drink —
So timid, while it lapped it seemed to shrink.

" Hard by, without the piny wood,
The stronghold grim was seen to brood
Above the misty sheet
That clung around its feet;
And when the partridge called its mate,
A train of thirty maidens stood
Before the frowning castle gate,
All robed in white, admission to await.

" 'Ho, there!' the warder from his tower;
'What seek ye, friends, at such an hour?'
'The warlike Turkoman,
Your ally, brave Osmân,'
The damsels cry, 'has gone to war;
And now we bid you grant the power
That we therein may safely bear
These treasures, which he trusteth to your care.

" With creak and clank that terrified
The silence, did the drawbridge slide;
The thundering echo rolled,
As though in fold on fold
Of surging air, through dark ravine,
And smote Olympus' shaggy side;

The frighted hawk in flight was seen,
When the procession, white and slow, passed in.

" When they had reached the inner keep,
    A yell, that made the cold skin creep, —
        A sharp and fiendish cry, —
        Went up the shuddering sky ;
    The figures doffed their woman's guise ;
    The garrison, awaked from sleep,
    Were seized with terrible surprise ; —
They saw Osmân the Turk before their eyes !

" There was no time to sue for life ;
    The foe drew forth the hidden knife ;
        And Mercy was not there,
        Afraid her raiment fair
    To soil in scene so sadly foul :
    'T was butchery, instead of strife ;
    Nor was there shrift for parting soul,
To soothe the passage to the spirit's goal !

" From their pale lips life scarce had flown,
    And scarce was hushed the dying groan,
        Ere to the torrent's flow
        That muttered far below,
    From the gray turret's dizzy height,
    The gasping murdered men were thrown ;
    And soon their faces, ghastly white,
Were shadowed by the vulture and the kite.

" Full twenty faithful hearts, or more,
　Were left to welter in their gore ;
　　The tower, in dreariness, —
　　A place for serpent's hiss,
　For wizard haunt and ghoul's demesne, —
　Osmân forsook the self-same hour,
　And hastened to the reedy fen,
In ambush to abide the festive train.

" And now the hour to go drew near,
　But the old crone, with many a tear. —
　　Elene's old withered nurse, —
　　Did fearfully rehearse
　How that, from neighboring cypress spire,
　The owl had filled her heart with fear
　The night before, — an omen dire
Of pending fate from Saints' disastrous ire.

"Though age more perfect knowledge brings
　To read the meaning of such things,
　　What recks of mystic tale
　　The warrior's heart of steel,
　And what the young, light-hearted maid ?
　They heeded not her counsellings :
　When twilight settled o'er the glade,
They quit the gates, a brilliant cavalcade.

" Oh, what a merry, joyous time !
　The tinkling brooks, with playful chime,

Danced o'er their pebbled beds,
Like sparkling silver threads
Broidered upon the myrtle spray;
The leaves' soft rustle seemed the rhyme
Of elfin sprites, whose magic lay
Has more of sweetness in the moonlight ray.

"And thus their palfreys ambled down
Gently through dell and grassy lawn;
And ever light and free
The notes of jubilee
Through darkling copse and forest rang;
And ever, as they wandered on,
Above the courser's hollow clang,
In chorus long and loud they laughed and sang.

"Anon their proud and champing steeds
Pace on through shadow-checkered meads,
Where rivulets meander
Bedecked with oleander;
And frequent ford, with radiant trail,
The warbling stream, whose pearly beads
With sparkling dew their forms engrail,
And spangle every warrior's chain-wrought mail.

"I travelled with them one sweet hour,
To where the willow wove a bower
With oak and olive wild,
And shadows soft beguiled

To hover quivering o'er the river ;
Then backward to my chieftain's tower,
Their music following on the zephyr,
I turned, and they were gone, and gone forever.

" That night, wrapped in my wool capote,
On yonder pile that stands remote,
While all did silence keep,
I vainly courted sleep ;
And gained, instead, the memory
Of what the beldame raved about
In her delirious prophecy,
To taunt me shivering superstitiously.

" I could not drive it from my mind.
Stranger, thou know'st the more inclined
Bad visions to forget
One is, the deeper set
They rankle in the tortured breast ;
And spite of will, my soul divined,
From signs on nature's face impressed,
That fearful hour was nigh, and rightly guessed.

" As said before, my simple bed
Upon the battlements was spread,
For this, the only reason,
That 't was the summer season ;
But as I gazed, bereft of sleep,
Upon the stars, a gradual shade,

A mist from southward, seemed to creep
With awful dimness o'er them, and to steep

" The atmosphere in mystic woe.
   The ghastly moon her face did show
      Cinctured by copper ring,
      Whose bale-portentous wing
   Encircled half the welkin vast;
   But not a breeze was heard to blow ;
   The forest's spirits, as they passed,
Feared to awake the leaves with phantom blast.

" No thing of life, no stirring form,
   Disturbed that stillness boding harm ;
      No jackal's dusky shade
      Glided across the glade,
   Nor heard the owlet's mournful call ;
   But, stricken by some threatening storm,
   Pale Nature owned a silent thrall,
As if the hand of Death had palsied all.

" The spell struck through my shuddering heart ;
   Alarmed, I shook, with frequent start,
      As though I felt the touch
      Of witch's icy clutch;
   Cold moisture dewed my forehead wan,
   My lips refused for prayer to part,
   Benumbed by fear's mysterious ban :
I longed to hear the voice of living man !

" In vain I sought the guard t' arouse,
    O'ercome by midday's hard carouse ;
        His features rough and stern
        Did towards the moon upturn ;
    He raved in sleep, and beat the air,
    As though he fought with mortal foes,
    And wist not of his wild nightmare :
I let him dream, and turned in dread despair

" Just then a breath —'t was scarce a breeze —
    Hovered amid the loftiest trees,
        And died before it blew;
        The cock in distance crew ;
    It was the third watch of the night :
    Grateful, I sank upon my knees,
    And sobbed, ' I thank thee, God of light,
There yet is life — 't was but a transient blight ! '

" While still in low obeisance bowed,
    It came ! — a roar like rushing flood
        Rumbled through depths profound
        Of mountains void of sound :
    A dreadful shudder broke the gloom ;
    And woods and cliffs, whose roots had stood
    A thousand years, now felt their doom,
And thundered from the heights with awful boom !

" At once the din of yelping fox,
    And myriad birds, in screeching flocks,

Whose cries bespoke distress,
Pierced through the wilderness,
With wailing voice and human yell!
Again the earthquake hurled the rocks;
A tower joined to the citadel
Heaved on its granite base, reeled, tottered, fell!

" Now blew the wind a soothing breath; —
So peace succeeds the pangs of death; —
Although a tremor rolled
At times along the wold;
Then did the warriors clamorous cry;
And some averred that, by their faith,
They saw Elene's pale ghost flit by,
And vanish straightway towards the misty sky.

" But while our hearts were terror-riven,
A piercing neigh shot up to heaven;
A horse, with loosened rein,
And wildly flying mane,
Dashed up the castle's craggy road:
His glossy hide was black as raven,
But it was stained with clotted blood,
And his keen eye gleamed fiercely where he stood.

" O Panayia![1] my heart doth bleed!
For when our youth, with timorous speed,

---

[1] The Virgin Mary.

Rushed to the postern gate,
Where he did restive wait,
And let the pawing charger in,
Behold, it was the tasselled steed
Which she had ridden like a queen,
With smiling rapture in her soft blue een.

" It was — it was her noble horse!
They swore so by the holy cross!
But where, oh, where was she?
In lone captivity?
Or lying on some distant plain,
A cold, neglected, tombless corse?
Ah, then they mourned in dismal strain,
With wail tumultuous, ' Elene! Elene!'

" And now, as morn drew on apace,
A soldier, wayworn, lank of face,
Arrived in weary haste
Where we stood all aghast,
And said, ' Lo, in the vale of pines,
In lonely, dark, and marshy place,
'Mid sighing sedge and trailing vines,
The gentle maiden's pallid corpse reclines.'

" The fugitive told us, with tears,
That they were singing, free of fears,
Beside the glassy stream,
When they beheld the gleam

Of glaring eyeballs in the dell ;
The riders fell by hidden spears, —
Even the bride, so fair and frail, —
And he alone escaped to tell the tale."

" And did they leave her lying there ? "
The traveller asks, with plaintive air.
  " Ah, no ! they sent a troop,
    Ere eve began to droop,
Of faithful horsemen to the wild,
Who brought her, still in death how fair !
Rose faintly hued her features mild ;
Half seemed as if her vanished spirit smiled.

" With violets blue they wreathed her brow,
And bid the solemn dirges flow,
    And washed her mournful bier
    With many a bitter tear :
It scarce could be a sin to rave,
When all our hearts were filled with woe,
To think, ah me ! we could not save
Our darling from the bleak and silent grave ! "

" Did Kara Yani, all forlore,"
The saddened stranger asks once more,
  " Grieve for his lovely daughter,
    Thus slain in ruthless slaughter ? "
" Deprive the eagle of her brood,
And will she not that very hour
Her head with listless pinion hood,
And pine her life away in sullen mood ?

" So when his child the chieftain lost,
    The treasure that he cherished most,
        Consumed by cankering care,
        He sought seclusion there ;
    But crying, in an evil hour,
  ' On battle-field I yield the ghost,'
    He fiercely quit his gloomy tower ;
The foe entrapped him and he came no more.

" There on its rocky pedestal,
    The thistle flaunting from the wall
        Its only banner now,
        And time its only foe,
    That dreary fortress silent stands ;
    Unheard the watchman's midnight call,
    Unheard the captain's loud commands,
Nor festive song, nor shout of martial bands.

" In summer time its shade affords
    A caravansary for herds
        Of the lone shepherd swain,
        Who pipeth mellow strain
    The livelong day amid the flowers,
    Whose parasitic beauty girds
    The lofty, gray, and mouldering towers,   [roars.
That gaze where Spring's foam-whitened torrent

" And there the passage birds alight,
    When winging on their southward flight,
        And sweeten Autumn's sadness
        With their shrill notes of gladness.
6

In those old bygone days I said,
In bitterness of soul, ' "T is right
That I, who loved the noble dead,
With frequent prayer should soothe their lonely bed.

" Therefore I solitary dwell
In this my wild and rock-hewn cell,
    And light my brushwood fire
    At night, with fear t' inspire
The wolf that prowls in search of prey ;
When loosened stones leap down the dell
From yonder ruin, and betray
That evil spirits aid its sad decay ; —

" When storm-blasts sweep, with wail prolonged,
Where mourning pines are densely thronged,
    Such season I am wont
    These holy beads to count,
And pray, as I recall the grace
Which to her saint-like face belonged,
That angels good may never cease
To guide her gentle spirit into peace.

" Now, traveller, hie thee ere the sun
Sink down behind yon mountains dun, —
    Ere night her shadows weave,
    The wanderer to deceive.
God speed thee on thy homeward way,
And may thy days rejoicing run !
For me sometimes if thou would'st pray,
It might, perchance, this simple tale repay."

PIETRO DELLA VALLÉ'S LAMENT.

PIETRO DELLA VALLÉ'S LAMENT.

LIKE one forlorn, from land to land
   The traveller wandered long;
But aye the touch of one soft hand,
   A voice of sweetest song,
Did haunt his dreams in broken sleep,
   And round his thoughts did wreathe
By day; and as he turned to weep,
   His bruiséd heart would breathe,
          " My fair Maâny :

" Where'er I stray, thy lovely form
   Goes with me, as whilome ;
But that sweet soul that had a charm
   To tinge thy cheek with bloom,
To fill that wild, dark eye of thine
   With love's resistless fire, —
Oh! could so bright a star decline,
   So soft a flame expire,
          My fair Maâny ?

" Return, sweet spirit, oh, return !
   Reänimate this clay !

By day and night for thee I mourn —
    Where does my birdling stray?
My heart nought else had learnt to own
    Than thee, when thou wert here;
And there's no balm since thou art gone
    To soothe the bitter tear,
              My fair Maâny.

" No more shall Mosellay's[1] green bowers,
    Nor dimpling Rocknebad,[2]
Nor gorgeous Bagdad's golden towers
    My sorrowing spirit glad :
The fleecy welkin greets my eye ;
    I hear the nightingale,
When summer winds go moaning by,
    Along the purple vale,
              My fair Maâny.

" But what are nature's beauties now,
    And what the world to me,
Whose eyes are dimmed with blackest woe,
    As though I could not see ?
Dark sorrow has eclipsed my joys,
    A grief I cannot flee :
And e'er I hear a hollow voice
    Whispering, ' Oh, where is she,
              Your lost Maâny?'

---

[1] A garden of Shiraz.   [2] A stream of Shiraz.

" How oft I dream thou hov'rest near,
　　To calm my frantic heart;
And 't is not all a dream, for here
　　(Alas, how still!) thou art.
And shall my sighs be all unheard,
　　Unheeded my emotion?
Oh, I am lonely as a bird
　　Upon the pathless ocean,
　　　　　　My fair Maâny!

" I may not wake thy soul again
　　To life's unceasing care;
To all the agony of pain
　　That haunts the dwellers here:
No! no! unbroken be thy rest;
　　I'll bear life's weary thrall
A few days more, since thou art blest,
　　My love — my hope — my all —
　　　　　　My own Maâny!"

SONNETS FROM THE ORIENT.

SMYRNA.

THE sunset gun has died along the sea;
It is the evening of Bairami's[1] fête;
The torches on each tapering minaret
Flash in the rippling waters of the bay,
And languid vapor dims the droning town :
From Smyrna's dewy gardens floats the scent
Of myrtle, rose, and citron, softly blent,
Like votive incense by each zephyr blown
Round the blind minstrel's[2] cave.   Since he began
His deathless song, weird city of the dead,
Aged Smyrna ! thou hast heard the busy tread
Of buried millions where the caravan
Now wends its tinkling way by Meles' stream,
Where ramparts moulder in the moonlight beam.

---

[1] A Turkish festival.   [2] Homer.

THE EGEAN.

TAYGETUS' snowy ridge, Tænarium's cape.
And Cythera's islet stretching far away,
Are purpled by the tints of dying day,
And the Egean heaves its glassy deep,
A tranquil mirror for the westering sun.
Time-hallowed Sea! — from shadowy isle to isle
Still echoeth faint the Lesbian lyre, erewhile
Blending with Doric song.   Aye! not alone
For what thou art, but for the deeds of worth
Done on thy shores, I love thy billows' roar,
Nor, exile-like, would leave thee evermore;
But as the bird that flies the wintry north,
And with the Spring re-seeks its native dell,
So bid I thee, Egean wave, farewell!

SICILY.

A PLEASANT land looms up against the sky;
Green hills and slopes, bright with perennial Spring,
And domes and airy spires, faint glittering
Through their light wreaths of seamist. greet the eye;
While, floating wildly o'er the deep-blue sea,
The boatman's music lulls th' enchanted ear.
Sicilia's island this, the sister fair
Who sweetly smiles on vine-clad Italy:
Alike the sharer of her sons of song,
Her black-eyed maids, her heroes and her arts;
And drunk alike with blood of patriot hearts,
She rises, phœnix-like, from tyrants' wrong.
And asks thee, traveller, if thy wandering een
Have ever gazed upon a lovelier scene.

NOTES.

PAGE 8. — *Their waving plumes and spectral steeds are gone.*

Scott's " Count Robert of Paris " presents a lively picture of the appearance of the first Crusaders at Constantinople, the sensation the rude, but chivalrous, warriors produced at the Byzantine court, and the wily arts of Alexius, — naturally a noble monarch, but reduced by circumstances to the practice of treachery.

PAGE 14. — *Here thoughtful solitude reigns undisturbed.*

The Seraglio has for three reigns been forsaken as a place of residence; its precincts, " with many a foul and midnight murder fed," are too melancholy even for the abode of royalty.

PAGE 19. — *Here stands a cankered brazen pillar.*

" The space between the *metæ,* or goals, was filled with statues and obelisks; and we may still remark a very singular fragment of antiquity — the bodies of three serpents twisted into one pillar of brass. Their triple heads had once supported the golden tripod, which, after the defeat of Xerxes, was consecrated in the temple of Delphi by the victorious Greeks." The heads of these serpents have long been broken off. According to Gibbon, Mohammed II. shattered them with his iron mace on the day when he captured the city. Lamartine and Von Hammer do not, however, allude to this circumstance. The remaining monuments of the Hippodrome are a tapering stone column, one hundred feet high, once plated with brass, and an obelisk transported from Egypt, in excellent preservation.

. PAGE 20. — *Until the deep-mouthed cannon's sullen boom.*

From one of the hills of the Bosphorus cannon proclaim to the city the first appearance of fire at the same time that heralds announce the intelligence through the streets. The fires of Stambûl possess a fearful significance, because they have been, and still are, the media for expressing the public dissatisfaction with the ruling ministry; such at least has been the case since the Ottomans entered the capital. Lamartine finely observes, " L'opinion publique asservie, mais indignée, se revela par des incendies multipliés dans Constantinople, avertissements ano·nymes qui prennent le feu pour voix, et soulèvent le peuple par la terreur et le désespoir." The conflagration raised by the Greens and Blues, when "the greatest tumult known in history" shook the throne of Justinian, the eight days' fire kindled by the Latin faction in 1203, and the combustion of twenty thousand houses in one night, in the reign of Selim II., are favorable specimens of the talent so often displayed by Constantinople in this line.

PAGE 26. — *And the foam-sheaf of fountains falls,*
From night to day, from day to night, etc.

" Day and night to the billow the fountain calls."
TENNYSON.

PAGE 29. — *Hangs upon the string a pearl.*

The idea of imparting to these pearls a sympathy with the fortunes of the island maidens was suggested by a tale read by the author in childhood.

PAGE 54. — *Explore the ocean bound with ice.*

The ladies of old time were only equalled in their exactions by the docility of their lovers. The romances and legends of the Middle Ages teem with examples. Out of numerous *authentic* cases behold one. It is told of Harold Harfager, one of the greatest kings of Norway, that he was coolly informed by Gilda, his lady-love, that the sole condition which would insure success to his suit was the possession of the Norwegian sovereignty! After ten long years of hard fighting, he won the sceptre and his bride.

PAGE 55. — *Alas for swan-necked Edith !*

Edith, the mistress of Harold II., of England, and the person who recognized his corpse on the battle-field of Hastings, was, on account of her charms, surnamed *swan-necked.*

PAGE 65. — *The Bride of Brusa.*

The scene of the plot being laid in that portion of Bithynia in which lies Brusa the Beautiful, the title is more appropriate than might at first appear. The poem was suggested by the following legend, related by Von Hammer: Osmân, the founder of the Ottoman Empire, when first building up his fortunes, formed a politic alliance with the lord of Biledjik. One article of the treaty was that Osmân, when he went to war, should have the liberty of depositing his treasures in the castle of his ally. After subduing the neighboring chieftains, he sought to seize Biledjik. An opportunity offered, on the departure of its unsuspecting master, to wed the daughter of a Greek chieftain. Osmân captured the castle by the stratagem described in the poem, and fell upon the bridal train. The bridegroom was slain, and Niloufer his bride given to Orchan, the son and heir of Osmân. It will be observed that some liberties have been taken with the legend, not so much to be deprecated, since even the historians present a woful discrepancy in their account of this affair. The earthquake is described from personal experience. The region of Brusa is notorious for its volcanic phenomena. Elene, the name of the heroine, and the Greek for Helen, is properly divisible into three syllables. It has been thought best partially to Anglicize it by silencing the last vowel.

Page 85. — *Pietro Della Vallé's Lament.*

Pietro Della Vallé, a celebrated Italian traveller of the seventeenth century, married a beautiful Nestorian lady of Bagdad, who accompanied him on his travels. At the age of twenty-one, death snatched her from his arms. A total change now came over the mind of Della Vallé, and a cloud, black as Erebus, descended upon his soul. He resolved that she should not be laid in Persia, where he could nevermore visit her grave. He therefore contrived to have the body embalmed; then, enclosing it in a coffin, placed it in a travelling-chest, that wherever destiny should guide him, the dear remains of his Maâny might accompany him to the grave.

Page 89. — *Round the blind minstrel's cave.*

' Seven places of antiquity were emulous for the honor of being the birthplace of Homer, the reputed son of Mæon. The claims of Smyrna were the most plausible. There, before setting out on his travels, he blended the bitter with the sweet, by undertaking the trials of schoolmaster, and paying his devotions to the Muses. Tradition still points to a cave in the vicinity of Smyrna as one of his favorite retreats.

www.ingramcontent.com/pod-product-compliance
Lightning Source LLC
Chambersburg PA
CBHW032201010726
47493CB00008BA/2782